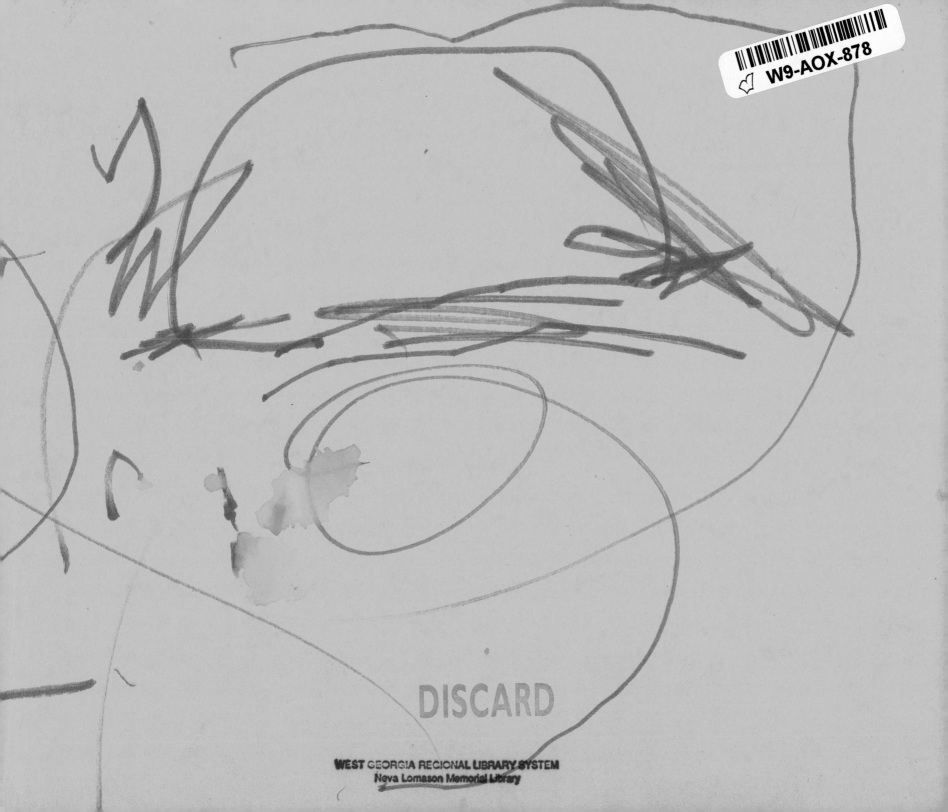

MUSKRAT, MUSKRAT, EAT YOUR PEAS!

Sarah Wilson

SIMON AND SCHUSTER BOOKS FOR YOUNG READERS

Published by Simon & Schuster Inc.

New York

For Rob, with love

Simon and Schuster
Books for Young Readers
Simon & Schuster Building
Rockefeller Center
1230 Avenue of the Americas
New York, New York 10020

SIMON AND SCHUSTER BOOKS FOR YOUNG READERS
is a trademark of Simon & Schuster Inc.

Designed by Lynn Fischer
Manufactured in the United States of America

10 9 8 7 6 5 4 3 2

Library-of-Congress Cataloging-in-Publication Data
Wilson, Sarah.
Muskrat, Muskrat, eat your peas!
Summary: After Muskrat's family meticulously plants, waters, and
harvests peas, Muskrat doesn't want any.
[1. Peas—Fiction.   2. Food—Fiction.   3. Muskrats—Fiction.]
I. Title.   PZ7.W6986Mu   [E]   88-29742

ISBN 0-671-67515-X

"Muskrat, Muskrat, eat your peas!"

"Remember how Uncle George and Cousin Walter planted the peas?

And how Great-Uncle Roger watered the peas?"

"And how Cousin Jesse and Cousin Jennifer
put up poles for the peas?

Remember how Uncle Ollie chased bugs away from the peas by day?"

"And how Uncle Sidney chased bugs away from the peas by night?

And how Uncle Buster sang to the peas?"

"Remember how Aunt Abigail
weeded the peas?

"OOOOF!"

And how Aunt Harriet and Cousin Willy
picked the peas?"

"And how Aunt Jessica and Uncle Stanley shelled the peas?

And now, Muskrat,

Great-Aunt Margery and Cousin Humphrey have
cooked the peas just right."

"So, Muskrat, Muskrat…eat your peas!"

"I know how hard you've all worked," said Muskrat. "But I don't *like* peas...

I'VE NEVER, EVER LIKED PEAS!"

"I HATE PEAS!"

"WHAT'S WRONG WITH PEAS?"

"PEAS MAKE ME SNEEZE."

"Now I've done it. They're all mad at me."

"They're going to send me home."

"MUSKRAT, MUSKRAT, EAT YOUR...

"You mean I don't have to eat peas?

Thank you!" said Muskrat. "Will you join me?"

"Of course!" said all of Muskrat's family.

And they did.

CHILDREN'S ROOM